Samuel French Acting Edition

Dontrell, Who Kissed the Sea

by Nathan Alan Davis

SAMUELFRENCH.COM   SAMUELFRENCH.CO.UK

FOR PRODUCTION ENQUIRIES

UNITED STATES AND CANADA
Info@SamuelFrench.com
1-866-598-8449

UNITED KINGDOM AND EUROPE
Plays@SamuelFrench.co.uk
020-7255-4302

Each title is subject to availability from Samuel French, depending upon country of performance. Please be aware that *DONTRELL, WHO KISSED THE SEA* may not be licensed by Samuel French in your territory. Professional and amateur producers should contact the nearest Samuel French office or licensing partner to verify availability.

MUSIC USE NOTE

Licensees are solely responsible for obtaining formal written permission from copyright owners to use copyrighted music in the performance of this play and are strongly cautioned to do so. If no such permission is obtained by the licensee, then the licensee must use only original music that the licensee owns and controls. Licensees are solely responsible and liable for all music clearances and shall indemnify the copyright owners of the play(s) and their licensing agent, Samuel French, against any costs, expenses, losses and liabilities arising from the use of music by licensees. Please contact the appropriate music licensing authority in your territory for the rights to any incidental music.

IMPORTANT BILLING AND CREDIT REQUIREMENTS

If you have obtained performance rights to this title, please refer to your licensing agreement for important billing and credit requirements.

DONTRELL, WHO KISSED THE SEA was first produced in a rolling world premiere by Skylight Theatre Company as a co-production with Lower Depth Theatre Ensemble (California), Phoenix Theatre Company (Indianapolis, Indiana), Theater Alliance (Washington, DC), Oregon Contemporary Theatre (Eugene, Oregon), and Cleveland Public Theatre as part of the National New Play Network's Continued Life Program. The Skylight Theatre Company (Gary Grossman, Artistic Director) and Lower Depth Theatre Ensemble (Gregg T. Daniel, Artistic Director) production opened in February of 2015, directed by Gregory Wallace. The cast was as follows:

DONTRELL JONES III . . . . Omete Anassi

ERIKA . . . . Hayley McHugh

DAD (DONTRELL JONES JR.). . . . . Marlon Sanders

MOM (SOPHIA JONES). . . . . Benai A. Boyd

DANIELLE. . . . . Jasmine St. Clair

ROBBY . . . . Charles McCoy

The Phoenix Theatre Company production opened in April of 2015, directed by Artistic Director Bryan Fonseca.

The Cleveland Public Theatre (Raymond Bobgan, Artistic Director) production opened in May of 2015, directed by Megan Sandberg-Zakian.

The Theater Alliance (Colin Hovde, Artistic Director) production opened in May of 2015, directed by Timothy Douglas.

The Oregon Contemporary Theatre (Craig Willis, Artistic Director) production opened in May of 2015, co-directed by Maya Thomas and Craig Willis.

DONTRELL, WHO KISSED THE SEA was presented in a developmental production at CULTURALDC's 2014 Source Festival (Jenny McConnel Frederick, Artistic Director) in Washington, DC, directed by Mark Hairston.

CHARACTERS

DONTRELL JONES III – (Male, Black, eighteen) Heir to a haunting and powerful legacy.

ERIKA – (Female, White, twenty-one) A lifeguard and Dontrell's soul mate.

DAD (DONTRELL JONES JR.) – (Male, Black, forties) Dontrell's father.

MOM (SOPHIA JONES) – (Female, Black, forties) Dontrell's mother.

DANIELLE – (Female, Black, seventeen) Dontrell's little sister.

SHEA – (Female, Black, thirties) Dontrell's cousin on his father's side.

ROBBY – (Male, Black, nineteen) Dontrell's best friend and an honorary member of the family.

SETTING

Baltimore, Maryland; the Chesapeake Bay coast; the Atlantic Ocean.

TIME

The present.

AUTHOR'S NOTES

An ellipsis in the dialogue (…) represents a pause, a beat, or perhaps a physical action.

A slash / marks the beginning of an overlap.

COMPANY/DESIGN

All actors except Dontrell are part of the Company. The Company can remain onstage for most of the play. Their physical placement and focus, presence, or absence visually underscores the action. When a character "enters" or "exits," this implies entering or exiting the defined space of the given scene.

Look toward representational and versatile set pieces that serve multiple uses.

As the visual narrator of the action, the Company helps to arrange the set and execute transitions. Transitions should be considered part of the play, rather than masked.

MOVEMENT/DANCE VOCABULARY

A choreographer with a background in African dance should be included as part of the creative team. In particular, look to incorporate the dance of Yemaya (Yemoja): Yoruba Goddess of the Ocean, Salt Water, Life and Fertility.

Likewise, someone with skill and knowledge in West African drumming can add an extra dimension to the production.

YORUBA LANGUAGE

There are lines at the end of the play that must be spoken in Yoruba. Please be sure to consult primary sources/Yoruba speakers to ensure that the language is expressed accurately.

SPECIAL THANKS

This play has found its way thanks to many, many dear friends and colleagues. My heartfelt thanks goes to everyone who has made Dontrell a part of their lives and helped it along. I would like to specially acknowledge the cast and production team at Indiana University's 2013 At First Sight Festival, where this play took its first steps into the world: Yusuf Agunbiade, Ian Martin, Elaine Griffin, Jordan Morning, Patricia Millard, Jasmine Desiree Traylor, Jessica Turner, Rachel Livingston, Rachael Fernandez, Haylie McClinn, Andrea Ball, Johna Sewell, Katie Gruenhagen, Derek Jones, Sandy Everett, Nicolette Apraez, Jeffrey Lindquist, and our fearless leader, Fontaine Syer.

Thank you to Ken Weitzman, without whose support and mentorship this play would not exist.

Thank you to Gavin Witt, whose dramaturgical support was instrumental in the growth of the script.

Thank you to Dane Figueroa Edidi, who choreographed two early productions and performed in one.

Thank you to Gregory Wallace for giving the play its final, essential push, and to NNPN, Skylight Theatre, and Lower Depth Theatre for their collaboration, which made that possible.

Thank you to Timothy Douglas for leading the deservedly well-acclaimed production at Theater Alliance.

Thank you to Fontaine Syer, whose passion for this play was as intense as my own. May *Dontrell, Who Kissed the Sea* help to honor her memory.

Prologue

*(The cast enters the playing space. The actor playing **DONTRELL** stands at center. The rest of the actors stand facing him in a wide circle or arc.)*

(Stillness.)

(A simple ritual. One at a time the actors in the **COMPANY** *approach* **DONTRELL**.*)*

ROBBY. *(Giving **DONTRELL** a mini-cassette recorder.)* Keep a record.

SHEA. *(Putting a cassette in the recorder.)* Speak it right.

DAD. *(Holding up a pair of very old shoes.)* Walk in these.

ALL COMPANY. Tread light.

ERIKA. *(Giving him a sip of water from a cup.)* A river for your thirst.

DANIELLE. *(Feeding him a piece of cake.)* Pack you a snack.

MOM. *(Tilting up his head by the chin.)* Eyes to the East:

ALL COMPANY. *(Claps their hands.) (Clap.) – (Clap.) – (Clap.)*

(A Great Sound: as of a giant monument crashing into the ocean.)

*(**COMPANY** disperses to the periphery of the stage.)*

(The Great Sound crescendos and finally halts.)

(Silence.)

Scene One

> (**COMPANY** *stomps on the ground four times.*)

ALL COMPANY. *(Thud.)*

…

> *(Thud.)*

…

> *(Thud.)*

…

> *(Thud.)*

> (**COMPANY** *sits and watches* **DONTRELL**. *He is in his room. It is late summer in Baltimore, Maryland. Very early morning.*)

> (**DONTRELL** *wakes from a vivid dream. He picks up a mini-cassette recorder, turns it on, and speaks into it. In doing so, he addresses the audience.*)

DONTRELL. Captain's log:

Future generations, whoever finds this: I hope it finds you well.

This Dontrell Jones the Third, of Baltimore. Spittin' to you live through space and time.

As your advanced technologies and mental-intuitive capacities may or may not allow you to decipher,

I'm in my PJs right now.

T-shirt and mesh. That's how I rest. But if I had known last night what I would dream…?!

DANIELLE. *(Heartbeats.)* Bum-bum.

SHEA. Pitter.

MOM. Patter.

DONTRELL. If I had known last night what I would dream…

ALL COMPANY. Heart-beat.

Heart-beat.

DONTRELL. I woulda put on a *suit* y'all, I'm *tellin'* you.

ERIKA. Deep breath.

ROBBY. One more.

DAD. One more.

DONTRELL. Just dreamt of a captive African, name
   unknown,
   One among a mass of tight-packed bodies,
   Swaying with the tide of the Atlantic,
   In the womb-like darkness of a slaver's vessel.
   Said African is alert. A cunning mind.
   I hear his shackles opening. I hear,
   A thud as his feet meet the floor –

ALL COMPANY. *(Lightly.) (Thud.)*

DONTRELL. And I can see him now: He has my father's
   face.
   I speak to him: "I am Dontrell Jones the Third.
   What is your name?" At this, he walks away.
   I trail his footsteps. He squeezes through a doorway.
   I follow him: And we are among the women.
   He taps one on the shoulder, she stirs.
   He tells her his name –
   – This dreamer did not hear it –
   She tells him hers –
   – Again, too low a whisper –
   For awhile they are silent.

MOM. Silent.

DAD. Silent.

DANIELLE. Silent.

DONTRELL. She speaks to him again.
   He climbs on top of her.
   She spreads her legs as best she can in her little cubby.
   They intertwine as best they can.
   They find each other's rhythm.
   Her fields cultivate themselves, and a little seed is
   nourished there.

They lie together. Man, woman and child.

In the darkness and the stench of the belly of the ship,

Floating on the freshness of the new moon sea.

Before sunrise, the man rises.

He climbs through a small hatchway to the deck. He stands tall on the wall of the ship.

With dawn approaching, the setting stars seem to cradle him.

He turns his head slowly to the right, then to the left.

He springs into the deep. As I rush to the ship's edge to give chase,

The cool air blows my eyes awake –

And I am here.

Dawn's early light at my window.

...

I'll let it in.

> (**DONTRELL** *gestures as if opening blinds or curtains. Soft light streams in.*)

DONTRELL. You hear that, future?

> (*Holds his recorder out to capture the silence.*)

A city that knows how to sleep.

But I may never rest soundly again:

How am I to answer this priceless vision?

Should I believe what I already think I know?

That it's now my burden to pull him up to shore?

> (**DANIELLE** *enters.*)

DANIELLE. Mama say come get breakfast, punk.

DONTRELL. *(Recorder off.)* That ain't cool, Danielle, you messin' up my Captain's Log.

DANIELLE. Whatever, just come on. She beatin' the shit out the eggs, you need to calm her down.

DONTRELL. How I'm s'pose to calm her down?

DANIELLE. Just come get breakfast. That's all I'm sayin'.

Don't make nobody come find you.

Don't make nobody twist your arm.

Just come sit at the table and eat. Alright?

DONTRELL. I'll come when I can.

DANIELLE. *D.*

DONTRELL. What I just said? I'll come as soon as I can.

DANIELLE. You know where Mama puts all her residual stress.

Me.

DONTRELL. I know.

DANIELLE. She don't think you gonna make it to campus.

She think somethin' crazy gonna happen before you start.

'Cause you ain't actin' right.

DONTRELL. Tell her I'll be there when I can.

> *(DANIELLE exits.)*

(Recorder on.) Future: I do not like eggs.

My mother, my sister,

Most definitely my father...

What would they say to me?

I'll have no breakfast.

> *(Readying himself to leave.)*

My cousin, Shea, knows a secret thing or two about the ocean,

And claims she knows me better than I know myself.

I'll go and put her expertise to work.

> *(Climbing out his window.)*

Out the window, then, and I'm off on foot.

> *(DONTRELL slowly raises his foot and takes a step. The first step of his journey. As his foot lands, the COMPANY stomps or pounds the stage.)*

ALL COMPANY. *(Thud!)*

DONTRELL. Future Generations, I presume
    That you will find my meditations crude,

> *(More steps follow...)*

ALL COMPANY. *(Thud!)*

DONTRELL. My insights blunt,

ALL COMPANY. *(Thud!)*

DONTRELL. And my aims short-sighted.

ALL COMPANY. *(Thud!)*

DONTRELL. My only hope in leaving you this record,

ALL COMPANY. *(Thud!)*

DONTRELL. Is to pass along those sparks of certain Truth,
    That even stones can make, if they be guided.

> *(Recorder off.)*

> **(DONTRELL** *now walks at a quicker pace.)*

COMPANY. *(Thud!) (Thud!) (Thud!) (Thud!) (Thud!)*

Scene Two

*(ROBBY enters. He stands or sits as if behind the
wheel of a car. He stares at DONTRELL.)*

ROBBY. *(Mockingly. Bob Marley.) Exodus. Movement of the
people.*
Look at this walkin-ass motherfucker.

DONTRELL. What's up, Rob.

ROBBY. Drivin' around looking for your vagrant ass is
what's up. Get in the car.

DONTRELL. I'm goin' to see Shea at her work.

ROBBY. So, do you get like extra points for goin' all Lewis
and Clark with the shit, or do you want a ride?

DONTRELL. *(Situates himself next to ROBBY.)* ...
Dude.
She works up at the Aquarium.
That way.

ROBBY. It's the long way not the wrong way. Recognize.

DONTRELL. Rob, I need to get up there, forreal.

*(ROBBY turns up the stereo. It's an instrumental
track*.)*

ROBBY. *Uh,*
This my jam right here. This my beat.
You ain't even heard this yet have you? See that's what
happens when you don't stay up, man, you miss the
fresh shit while it's fresh. So wassup, you wanna jump
on this track?
You got a verse?

DONTRELL. ...

(ROBBY turns the music up louder.)

ROBBY. *(Easing into the rhythm.)*

---

*Licensees should create original music or use music in the public
domain.

ALRIGHT I'LL START IT OFF, I'LL START IF OFF, LET YOU
    ACCLIMATE.
UH, HOLD IT DOWN LIKE A PAPER WEIGHT.
UH, PASS OUT JUST TO RESUSCITATE.
UH, YO,
CHECK IT:
EARLY BIRD BUT AIN'T NO WORM,

    (Taking a hard right.)

ROBBY.

JUST LEAN INTO THE TURN,
I FIGURE EIGHT YOUR INNER HARBOR
MY RHYMES MAKE YOU SEE FARTHER,
AND THIS JUST THE A.M. I AIN'T EVEN AWAKE
OH, LOOK THERE GO THE SUN,
CHARM CITY SLEEPS IN, BUT WE GET IT DONE,
OLD BUILDINGS WE REFURBISH 'EM
OLD DESIGNS WE RE-PURPOSE 'EM,
WE THE MASON AND THE DIXON,
WHERE THEY BROUGHT SLAVE SHIPS IN,
WALKIN' OVER PRISONS
GHOSTS BENEATH THE STREETS,
AND THEY WONDER WHY WE STRIDE
JUST A LITTLE OFF THE BEAT.
UH
MY GUY D GONNA LET Y'ALL HAVE IT,
BRACE YOURSELVES,
HE GONNA BRING THAT NERDY MAGIC:

    (ROBBY *looks at* **DONTRELL,** *nodding his head.)*

    (DONTRELL *turns the music down.)*

DONTRELL. That was dope.

Ghosts beneath the streets. What made you say that?

ROBBY. Just comin' off the top of the dome, man. You
    fuckin' up the vibe talkin' about it, come on. Ain't you
    gonna jump on this beat?

This a dope beat. It's early as hell and I'm *hyped* that's a
    dope beat, you can't jump on this beat?

DONTRELL. *(Re:* **ROBBY**'s *driving.)* Rob, circle back around, man.

ROBBY. Oh, okay, I see. I see what this is:

Hopkins.

Right, player?

DONTRELL. What?

ROBBY. You get into Hopkins, you too good to hang out all summer.

DONTRELL. Rob, man, I'm not *even* thinkin' about school / right now –

ROBBY. Course you ain't *thinkin'* about it 'cause you don't have to, you a player. That's how y'all *do*. All the way back to Johns himself.

Johns Pimpjuice,

"YeahYouHeardRightMyIsPluralMotherfuckers CauseIgotItLikeThat" Hopkins.

Forreal that's what it says on the *degree*.

I ain't mad, though. MORGAN STATE!

BIG BAD BEARS ALL DAY!

BEST MOVE OUT THE WAY!

DONTRELL. School ain't no object, man.

ROBBY. What, then?

I'm not circling back for shit 'til you decide to come clean with a brother.

What's up with the aquarium?

What, you tryna be a Marine Psychologist or somethin'?

DONTRELL. …

ROBBY. Don't be lookin' at me like that I *go* to college alright?

DONTRELL. Never heard of no Marine / Psychologist before.

ROBBY. Yeah well maybe it's a new field, Johnny Hops, you ever think of that?

DONTRELL. You took a class in it?

ROBBY. Yes I did as a matterafact.

DONTRELL. You took a / Marine Psychology class?

ROBBY. Marine Psysology class, yes I did, boy-genius, thank you, yes I did.

    (A beat.)

You actin' *weird*, D.

DONTRELL. According to who?

ROBBY. According to you.

When a beat come on, you s'pose to come in with a broken ass, corny, nonsensical, Dontrellistic verse.

When I give you shit about your academics you s'pose to come back at me.

That's how we *do.*

DONTRELL. So I'm s'pose to be the same person my whole life? What's the point of that?

Hold up.

    (Taking out his recorder and turning it on.)

Captain's Log:

Future Generations, if I could,

I would die with every exhalation,

Then each breath taken in would be re-birth.

And I'd invent myself brand new again and again and again.

Is that how y'all do it, future?

    (Recorder off.)

ROBBY. …

Bro. You got your moms *trippin'*, bro. Forreal. She called me on the celly this mornin', D. Says I need to come over, drags me into the house and sits me down and makes me eat some burnt up eggs. And the whole time she just nonstop grilling me with all these questions about you. "Where Dontrell go this morning? What girls is he talkin' to? Why he can't sit down for meals?" And all I can say is, "Ma'am I don't know."

Your sister all quiet.

Your pops snoring loud as hell from the bedroom. Most awkward, depressing meal I've ever had. Except for that time me and you made them Robitussin shakes, that was / prolly worse –

DONTRELL. ...

>*(Steps out of the car.)*

'Preciate the lift, brother.

ROBBY. 'Ey.

Tell Shea I said what's up with Dontrell.

>*(**ROBBY** exits. **DONTRELL** walks into the aquarium.)*

ALL COMPANY. *(Thud!) (Thud!) (Thud!) (Thud!) (Thud!)*

Scene Three

(The National Aquarium, Baltimore.)

(DONTRELL *looks up at a huge tank of colorful, tropical fish.)*

(COMPANY [ERIKA] *is a clown fish [Nemo].)*

(DONTRELL *taps the glass.)*

DONTRELL. *(Tapping.)* Where you think you goin', Nemo? 'Ey,

'Ey, I'm talkin' to you, little fishy what's up?

Your daddy's lookin' for you, Nemo.

> **(ERIKA** *swims up to the glass and looks right at* **DONTRELL.***)*

Don't ever lose hope, little guy.

He'll come for you.

Promise he will.

Might seem like some impossible shit to you now. But he comin'.

That's what family does for family.

Right?

Wanna talk about some *Mission Impossible?*

Huh?

Wanna talk about some double-o-seven?

Yo, James Bond ain't got nothin' on your old man. James Bond never escaped through a *sink.* That's some straight up magic right there.

Your old man is like all the James Bonds put together, plus a Gandalf.

> **(ERIKA** *floats away.)*

Make good choices, lil bro. See you on the flip.

…

> **(DONTRELL** *taps the glass a few more times.)*

(Recorder on.)

Future generations, now that I reflect:
The water, the sound of it, even the thought of it,
Has always given me a sense of calm.
Of peace.
But now it is far more than that.
It stirs a muffled whisper in my veins.
But stand by, here comes my interpreter.

(Recorder off.)

(SHEA enters.)

'Sup, cuz? Been way / too long.

SHEA. Boy we ain't even open yet how you gonna infiltrate my place of work?

DONTRELL. Shea, I got urgent / matters to discuss, forreal.

SHEA. Up here tappin' the glass, don't none of these fishes speak no Morse Code.

DONTRELL. What *do* they speak?

SHEA. Oh, okay, look who's askin' me!

DONTRELL. You tellin' me what they don't speak / I'm askin' you what they speak –

SHEA. You s'pose to know things, cousitron. Don't let 'em find out you askin' *me* with my associates degree, might take away your scholarship. *And* your clunky-ass 8-track player.

DONTRELL. This a mini-cassette / ain't no 8-track

SHEA. *(Cracking up.)* Ha-haaaa!!

DONTRELL. You be playin' too much, Shea, / I'm here to talk.

SHEA. D, you know you come up in here tryna use a *tape deck* / I'ma talk about you –

DONTRELL. Ain't no tape deck neither I know my gadgets. This a journalistic tool, alright?
This here is for them old school cats that like to feel the tape rollin' when they patrollin'.

This is for Gangsta Journalists.

This a forreal account.

...

    (Recorder on.)

DONTRELL. Future, I'm here with Shea: Would you state your full name, please?

SHEA. Shea "I see what I see" Jones.

DONTRELL. Great, / and –

SHEA. And for the record, D,

I ain't no psychic.

...

...

DONTRELL. *(Recorder off.)* I was with my ancestor. Just a couple hours ago.

Our ancestor, Shea.

He looked like my dad.

SHEA. He looked like Uncle D?

DONTRELL. Spitting image.

SHEA. Okay.

DONTRELL. He was on his way over here. Across the ocean, knowhatimsayin'?

SHEA. Okay... D, listen –

DONTRELL. I don't *have* dreams like that. I barely ever *remember* my dreams, Shea. I mean that's gotta *mean* somethin'. That's gotta be a *message*. Right?

SHEA. What'd Uncle D say?

...

What did your father say, Dontrell?

DONTRELL. I ain't say nothin' to him yet.

SHEA. Why don't you?

DONTRELL. I need to talk to somebody who might actually *believe* me first, knowhatimean?

SHEA. ...

DONTRELL. When the time is right, I'm sure we'll have a sit down.

I'm sure we'll talk about it.

SHEA. Let me know how that goes.

DONTRELL. But what do *you* think about it Shea?

I'm here askin' *you*.

SHEA. …

One piece of advice from me, okay? And that's all.

DONTRELL. Thank you.

　　　(Recorder on.)

SHEA. I'ma tell you what I'm about to tell all these visitors when the doors open:

Don't forget what's around you.

Everyone wants to see the dolphins.

Everyone wants to get tropical and let their kids talk to Nemo. And that's fine.

But start where you at.

The Blue Crab. The Diamondback Terrapin. The Striped Burrfish.

Prepare to be Amazed,

By what's already around you.

Love what's around you.

There's no place like home.

Do you even know how true that is?

Look, I'm not gonna talk you through things anymore.

I'm not gonna walk you through scenarios,

I'm not gonna interpret dreams.

Be your own soothsayer.

Or find a professional.

If I can help you in a more practical way, let me know.

DONTRELL. *(Recorder off.)* Do you have access to scuba gear?

SHEA. To who?

DONTRELL. A mask, a wet suit, flippers, the whole nine.

You can't get a hookup from one of your coworkers or
something? Come on, I seen people in them tanks with
scuba gear on.

SHEA. They're trained divers, Dontrell. Can you even swim?

DONTRELL. …

Look, I'm gonna take a walk to the pool right now and
give myself a lesson. / Right now okay –

SHEA. Which pool?

DONTRELL. First one I get to. And you can just drop the
gear off at the crib when you get off work.

SHEA. …

DONTRELL. *(Recorder on.)* Future Generations:

There's many things I don't yet know.

But what I can tell you certainly is this:

I'll leave no deed undone

To save you from the haunts of history.

My liberty is bondage if I don't.

Shout out to my cousin Shea for her assistance.

Shea, for the record,

Will you help me get some gear?

(Holds out recorder.)

SHEA. …

…

Scene Four

(COMPANY creates Erika's apartment, the early morning sun shines through a large window. Sitting at her mirror, ERIKA puts on a few touches of makeup from a vintage-looking makeup case.)

ERIKA. First prerequisite of a True Lifeguard: Dedication.

Rise before the sun does.

Ready yourself. Because this day will be the day. That you are needed.

Don't *believe. Know.* That this is the day.

Until it isn't. And when it isn't: Rest well for tomorrow.

This is the sign of perfect dedication.

Second prerequisite:

Skallent.

What it sounds like.

Skill plus talent.

Because neither one likes to act alone.

Train, practice, meditate, excavate.

These are the actions of the Skallented.

Third prerequisite...

...

Third prerequisite.

Of a True Lifeguard.

...

A life.

A life to save.

This, always, is beyond your control.

You may guard lives with all your faithfulness,

For a thousand years,

And never taste the bliss,

Of a life renewed.

This is not a path to follow for the wrong reasons.

This is not a path to follow because you think you look good in a swimming suit.

This is not a path to follow because you want to forge
your own young-adult identity independent of your
exceptionally dysfunctional and uniquely damaged
family,

Because this is a path of no identity,

Because to give your breath to another,

Is an act that, in the end, must be entirely empty of self.

And so you empty yourself.

As best you can.

Every day.

> (**ERIKA** *looks out the window. It's brighter now.*)

ERIKA. Today's the day.

Today's the day.

Today

Is

The day.

> (**ERIKA** *exits.*)

Scene Five

(**COMPANY** *creates a swimming pool.*)

(**DONTRELL** *stands at the edge.*)

(**ERIKA** *enters and mounts a high lifeguard chair.*)

(**DONTRELL** *looks at the water.*)

DONTRELL. *(Recorder on.)* Future generations...

ALL COMPANY. Heart-beat. Heart-beat. Heart-beat.

ROBBY. Bum-bum.

SHEA. Pitter.

DAD. Patter.

DONTRELL. Mind over matter.

Talk to ya soon.

> *(Recorder off.)*

> (**DONTRELL** *places his recorder on the ground.*)

The fearless never fail.

ROBBY. Bum-bum

DONTRELL. My heart's the ship my mind's the sail.

SHEA. Bum-Bum

DONTRELL. It's the deep end today, tomorrow the whales.

> (**DONTRELL** *plugs his nose, jumps, and disappears.*
> *Stillness.*)

ALL COMPANY. Heart-beat.

Heart-beat.

Heart-beat, heart-beat, heart-beat!

> (**ERIKA** *looks down.*)

> *(Beat.)*

> *(She goes in after him.)*

MOM. Flai-ling.

DANIELLE. Pass out.

> (*ERIKA comes up with* DONTRELL. *She drags him out, lays him down. His eyes are closed. She puts her head to his chest.*)

ROBBY. Heart… Beat.

SHEA. Beat.

DANIELLE. Beat.

> (*ERIKA checks* DONTRELL*'s air passage. She blows into his mouth.*)
>
> (DONTRELL *coughs out water. Breathes in, wheezes, breathes in deeper.*)
>
> (DONTRELL *sits up.* DONTRELL *and* ERIKA *look at each other.*)

ALL COMPANY. Uh-oh.

> (DONTRELL *and* ERIKA *continue to look at each other.* COMPANY *gives them towels, which they drape over their shoulders.*)

ERIKA. Why'd you jump in if you don't know how to swim?

DONTRELL. I thought I could do it.

ERIKA. What made you think that?

DONTRELL. I made myself think it.

ERIKA. Oh.

DONTRELL. Mind over matter.

ERIKA. You're s'pose to start in the shallow end.

DONTRELL. Oh.

ERIKA. You have the body of a swimmer.

DONTRELL. Forreal?

ERIKA. Yup. You could probably be really good.

DONTRELL. Forreal?

ERIKA. Yeah.

DONTRELL. Why you sayin' that?

ERIKA. 'Cause it's true. 'Cause I noticed it.

DONTRELL. You ain't bullshittin'?

ERIKA. Nope.

DONTRELL. My name's Dontrell.

ERIKA. Pretty name.

DONTRELL. Thanks.

ERIKA. I'm Erika.

DONTRELL. Erika. That's wassup.

ERIKA. …

DONTRELL. *(Recorder on.)* Captain's log. I was made to be a swimmer.

This according to the testimony of an expert in the field.

Rio 2016[*], you heard it here first.

Say what's up to the future, Erika.

> *(**DONTRELL** holds the recorder near **ERICA**'s face.)*

ERIKA. …

Are you okay?

DONTRELL. *(Recorder off.)* Yeah, no, sorry, this just my captain's log.

ERIKA. No light-headedness?

DONTRELL. Naw.

ERIKA. You have to go to the doctor if you feel weird.

…

I have to tell people that.

DONTRELL. Will you be my swim coach?

ERIKA. Okay.

DONTRELL. Give me lessons?

ERIKA. Okay.

DONTRELL. When you wanna start?

ERIKA. Whenever.

DONTRELL. Soon?

ERIKA. Sure.

DONTRELL. Wanna hear somethin' outa this world?

---

[*]May be updated to the city and year of the next scheduled Summer Olympics.

ERIKA. Of course.

DONTRELL. I think I wrote a poem for you.

ERIKA. ...

DONTRELL. I didn't know it was for you.

I didn't know who it was for.

But I wrote it anyway.

ERIKA. Can I hear it?

DONTRELL. You sure you want to?

ERIKA. I think so.

DONTRELL. Alright...

> *(Slam poetry style.)*

Fuck Romeo and Juliet.

Star crossed lovers? Not so fast.

They were the stars, and love crossed *them.*

Lost their orbits for some ass.

But when we touch, my love and I,

Galaxies align.

Love wishes it could kiss like us,

And it'll learn in time.

But 'til it do, tell punk-ass Cupid to put his bow away.

All I want is you.

Love's clumsy feet would just get in the way.

ERIKA. ...

...

Deja vu.

DONTRELL. Really?

ERIKA. *(Getting kind of freaked out.)* Whooooa my God it's still happening.

DONTRELL. Did I do this:

> *(Does some random, impromptu movements.)*

...

...

ERIKA. No.

Thanks, I was kind of getting freaked out.

DONTRELL. No problem.

ERIKA. …

My shift's over.

…

DONTRELL. Oh, cool.

…

Where you headed now?

ERIKA. Down the Chesapeake. Eastern bay.

DONTRELL. I ain't been down the Bay in a minute.

ERIKA. Come on, then.

DONTRELL. Yeah?

ERIKA. If you want to.

DONTRELL. *(Recorder on.)* Captain's Log:

From the deep end to the Bay.

The path I tread is like no other way.

> (**COMPANY** *takes off the lifeguard chair and takes away the pool.*)
>
> (**DONTRELL** *and* **ERIKA** *exit.*)

Scene Six

> *(The Jones's living room.)*
>
> *(**COMPANY** brings on [or creates] a couch and a TV frame.)*
>
> *(**MOM** watches TV.)*
>
> *(**ACTOR GUY** and **ACTOR GIRL** [**ROBBY** and **DANIELLE**] are behind the TV frame having a moody, intense TV moment. Music underscores their scene as **MOM** watches.)*

ACTOR GIRL. The only place I want to be, Damien…the only place I've ever wanted to be…is with you.

ACTOR GUY. Don't say that.

ACTOR GIRL. But it's what I FEEL!!

> *(A knock at the front door.)*

SHEA. *(At the door.)* Anybody home?

MOM. *(Shouting loud as hell.)* COME IN!

> *(**SHEA** comes in holding a large bag.)*

ACTOR GUY. Listen to me. You're going to walk away.

ACTOR GIRL. No.

ACTOR GUY. You're going to live a good life.

ACTOR GIRL. You *are* my good life!

ACTOR GUY. Courtney, no. You don't understand.

SHEA. Is D around, Auntie Soph?

ACTOR GIRL. …I want to be your companion, Damien.

> *(Baring her neck.)*

Forever.

MOM. *(Giving up on the TV.)* Oh my God.

ACTOR GUY. You don't know what you're saying!

ACTOR GIRL. Yes I do.

MOM. Y'all are just, mmm mmm no.

ACTOR GUY. I love you too much, Courtney.

I could never…never…

ACTOR GIRL. I want you to.

ACTOR GUY. No… No… I…

ACTOR GIRL. Infect me! Infect me Damien! PLEASE!

MOM. *(Turning off the TV.)* That's enough of that shit.

        (COMPANY takes the TV frame away.)

SHEA. Is D around, auntie?

MOM. I *work,* okay?

SHEA. Yes ma'am.

MOM. You know how stressful it is to work for the public?

SHEA. Yes I do, / actually.

MOM. No no no, because see people like the aquarium. Okay? At least you dealin' with people who are somewhere they wanna be. People who are there by preference – don't ask me why 'cause most of them fishes ugly that's why God put 'em way the fuck down there outa sight, but hey, that's they cupatea.

You servin' people they cupatea you way ahead of the game already I don't feel sorry for you.

I got people crying, I'm sayin' flat out crying to me like children, every day "I just want the boot removed from my car and no one will help me!!" Well guess what, I can't help you that's not my department.

Every day.

Crying. Yelling.

And I come home, Shea, and I got a house to keep, got schedules to coordinate, got bills I can't even look at let alone pay, got A HUSBAND WHO WANTS TO TELL ME HE'S PLANNING TO RETIRE!!

        (DAD sits in his own room behind a door, the flickering lights of his TV on his face.)

DAD. *(Yelling from behind his door.)* Hey are you watching this?!

Dude finally bit her!

MOM. …

And I come home and I have maybe an hour, Shea.
Maybe an hour that I can unwind. At the most. And I
PAY for my cable, okay?

And I gotta spend my hour watching that mess?

That should be a punishable crime I'm more stressed
out now than when I sat down, what good is that?

…

(Registering **SHEA** *'s bag. Unimpressed.)* You brought me a
present?

SHEA. It's something Dontrell asked me for.

He's not around?

MOM. Ain't seen him today.

SHEA. Oh.

MOM. …

What's he up to, Shea?

SHEA. I don't really know.

MOM. How can you not worry yourself sick over your
children?

How?

He's a good kid.

Smart.

Got himself on full scholarship, can you believe it?

When things are going this well, Shea,

Cue the bad shit. Am I right?

Ain't that life?

Winter then Spring. Summer then Fall.

Ain't it?

SHEA. You ain't wrong.

MOM. The men on your side of the family, Shea.

Can only hold it together so much.

Prone to sabotage themselves.

And he startin'.

You don't think I know it when I see it?

Been prayin' since June for school to start.

My one prayer: Just get him there.

Get him started, let him find a spark, let him find a major, let him find a nice little college girlfriend, somethin'. And he'll be on his way.

Three weeks left and still I'm beggin'. Just get him there.

But why do I feel like I'm prayin' for the sun not to set?

(**SHEA** *puts the bag down.*)

SHEA. ...

Love you Auntie Soph.

(**SHEA** *exits.*)

(**MOM** *takes the scuba gear out of the bag and holds it up.*)

MOM. ...

...

DANIELLE COME HERE PLEASE!

(**DANIELLE** *enters.*)

We havin' a graduation party tomorrow I need you to plan it.

DANIELLE. For who?

MOM. For your *brother.*

DANIELLE. He had a party in May. When he graduated.

MOM. We havin' another one. Just for family.

DANIELLE. Tomorrow.

MOM. Yes.

I want you to call Robby.

DANIELLE. Why?

MOM. He's family –

DANIELLE. No he's not –

MOM. Want you to bake a cake,

Want you to get ahold of your brother and make sure he comes.

DANIELLE. …

What's goin' on with the flippers?

MOM. …Call Robby, bake the cake, make sure your brother comes.

DANIELLE. What kind of cake?

MOM. …

Don't matter. But make sure you decorate it. Make it beautiful. Alright?

DANIELLE. Yes ma'am.

MOM. We need to wake that boy up. You hear me?

DANIELLE. Yes, ma'am.

(**MOM** *exits.*)

Scene Seven

(Erika's condo. Beachfront, Chesapeake Bay.)

DONTRELL. I thought we was goin' sight seeing or something.

You *live* on the bay, that's wild.

ERIKA. It's just a place.

DONTRELL. Spacious.

ERIKA. Yeah.

DONTRELL. You stay here by yourself?

ERIKA. Uhuh.

DONTRELL. The mighty Chesapeake.

ERIKA. Yup.

DONTRELL. Private beach out there?

ERIKA. It's shared with the whole building.

But yeah. I never use it.

DONTRELL. Charm City charmed you that much, huh?

ERIKA. What?

DONTRELL. 'Cause that's a long-ass drive to work.

ERIKA. Well. I'm a real-ass lifeguard.

It's just a beauty contest down here, I can't stomach it.

DONTRELL. They give you like a commission or somethin' if you save a life?

ERIKA. ...

No.

DONTRELL. I'm playin'.

ERIKA. Ha-ha.

DONTRELL. ...

ERIKA. What do you want to drink? Water? That's all I have.

DONTRELL. Definitely.

ERIKA. I don't even have ice, sorry about that.

DONTRELL. Not a problem.

(ERIKA gives DONTRELL a glass of water. He drinks.)

You ever gone deep sea diving before?

ERIKA. Nope. I hear it's crazy down there.

DONTRELL. After my swimming lessons, can that be next?

ERIKA. …

    …

  How old are you?

DONTRELL. Eighteen.

  You?

ERIKA. You're not s'pose to ask but twenty-one.

DONTRELL. You're not s'pose to ask an old woman, you
  can ask a young woman.

ERIKA. If you know she's young. I could be any age.

DONTRELL. …

ERIKA. Yesterday was my twenty-first birthday, actually.

DONTRELL. Happy birthday.

ERIKA. Thanks. We can have left over cake for dinner. I
  have a lot of it, 'cause I don't have any friends.

DONTRELL. Oh.

ERIKA. I'm mostly kidding.

DONTRELL. Cool.

ERIKA. You know, I gave myself a birthday present.
  And it was to not question the things I see.
  And the things I know to be true.

DONTRELL. That's a really beautiful present.

ERIKA. …

  Let's have a sleepover, okay?
  We'll build a fort, then have cake.

       (Getting up.)

  Here, help me with this.

       *(**ERIKA** and **DONTRELL** make a small fort out
       of sheets. The **COMPANY** holds it over them like a
       canopy.)*

       *(All the lights are turned off, except for a flashlight,
       which **ERIKA** holds.)*

  Okay: Spotlight. You ready?

DONTRELL. What's spotlight?

ERIKA. It's,

Okay, I'll go first.

(Handing **DONTRELL** *the flashlight.)*

Here, you hold this.

So you're gonna shine the flashlight on my face. That's the spotlight. And the way it works is, it's a trust game. It's kind of like a psycho-emotional version of hot yoga – in that it could be potentially damaging. But it's a trust game, so danger is necessary. So basically, you shine the spotlight on my face and I have to tell you a secret.

DONTRELL. Okay.

ERIKA. And as long as you keep the spotlight on, I have to keep talking.

DONTRELL. Okay.

ERIKA. And I can't just talk. I have to talk forreal. Like tell you more and more of my secret until you decide to let me stop.

DONTRELL. Okay.

ERIKA. And then I do the same thing to you.

DONTRELL. Okay.

ERIKA. Oh. And it has to be not just like, information, but a secret. Something that you kinda don't want to talk about. 'Cause that's the whole point.

DONTRELL. Right.

ERIKA. Okay.

Okay.

Okay go ahead whenever.

*(***DONTRELL*** *shines the flashlight in* **ERIKA**'s *face.)*

Okay okay ohmyGodohmyGod, okay,

Oh my God I can't yes I can okay.

I've seriously never said this out loud before.

Okay my dad is my uncle.

DONTRELL. What?

ERIKA. I know, it's seriously fucked up, so fucked up, God. God, okay, so my mom cheated on my dad with his brother. And it's this huge family secret and I didn't find out until a year ago and it completely destroyed me, and the thing is that I didn't even know he *existed* until I was like twelve. Nobody told me he *existed* until I found some old picture in the basement. "Who's that, Mom?" "That's your father's brother." "Oh." So, yeah. Eight years later, he's my dad. And my uncle. I call him my duncle. Just to myself, in my head. I've never met him face to face.

...

Don't take the light away.

DONTRELL. Okay.

ERIKA. Now that it's out he calls a lot to check up on me. Which feels nice but also sometimes really weird. *Really* weird. And I told him I was planning to move out of my parents' place and he just *bought* me this condo. He put it in my name and everything. My mom didn't want me to move out but there was just...no way.

So what I do is I think about her in the morning. When I'm getting ready for the day. I use her old makeup case which I stole from her which was actually my grandma's and she's a can of worms that I couldn't even begin to open if I tried, so I *don't*, and... Lifeguarding is the thing that's kept me going. The hope that one day maybe I would save someone's life and maybe when I did they would also breathe new life into me. And I didn't literally breathe you back to life, but I still feel kind of like I did, and I'm starting to learn that things mean different things than you think and when the things that you hope are going to happen *do* happen they happen in different ways than you think they will and I'm just...really happy right now.

...

...

(**DONTRELL** *moves the light off of her face.*)

DONTRELL. …

…

You okay?

ERIKA. I feel really really good.

Thank you.

…

I'm good.

…

Thank you.

DONTRELL. Sure thing.

ERIKA. *(Taking the flashlight.)* Your turn, are you ready?

DONTRELL. I don't know.

ERIKA. I'll help you if you need it, okay?

…

Ready?

*(***ERIKA*** shines the light on ***DONTRELL****'s face.)*

DONTRELL. …

I've had this dream…

And I've had this thought…

ERIKA. What kind of dream?

DONTRELL. Powerful dream.

ERIKA. Okay…

DONTRELL. About a slave ship…

ERIKA. Keep going, Dontrell!

DONTRELL. I saw this one man in particular, that looks like
    my father… It was like he was… He got away. Kind of.
    And he threw himself into the ocean.

But his child made it over here.

And so he lived on. In a way.

He's my ancestor.

Direct line type of thing.

And I've felt this urge to go out, go out to the ocean
    and just…go see him, I guess. And I'm kinda worried
    'cause I got this text from my sister sayin' I need to

come home tomorrow afternoon for like a family…
thing…and I think maybe my cousin said something to
my mom, and basically I just… You know I don't know
if they're gonna believe me when I tell 'em.

Especially my dad.

He might think I'm losin' it or somethin'. Which maybe
I am…but then also a lot of things are starting to make
sense the more that I think about 'em. Like he wouldn't
teach my sister and me to swim and whenever we asked
him he always said he didn't know how…but he was in
the Navy for seven years?

And I think there's some things that have been hidden
from me.

But even if they stay hidden, they're operational.

And even if I don't know why I have to do certain
things… I can't not do them. You know, you can take
away all the reasons but you still have the causes.

And this is really something I'm s'pose to do.

Not just for me.

Or for my family even.

But as my contribution. To civilization.

That's what my captain's log is for, too. My tape. So
there's a record.

I didn't ask for none of this.

But there it is.

That's why I'm tryna learn to swim.

That's why I was at the pool.

That's why I met you.

…

…

(**ERIKA** *turns off the flashlight.*)

ERIKA. Do you believe in spirits?

DONTRELL. Do you?

ERIKA. I always have.

DONTRELL. Me too.

ERIKA. Can I come closer?

DONTRELL. Yes.

> (**DONTRELL** *and* **ERIKA** *are silhouetted in blue. The ocean surges outside the window.*)
>
> (**ERIKA** *straddles* **DONTRELL**.)

ERIKA. I think you're very brave.

DONTRELL. I think so are you.

ERIKA. I think you're my hero.

DONTRELL. You saved my life.

ERIKA. I'll let you make it up to me.

DONTRELL. You're strong.

ERIKA. Uhuh.

DONTRELL. You're a woman.

ERIKA. Sometimes.

DONTRELL. You're a Viking.

ERIKA. *(Laughing.)* Not exactly.

DONTRELL. Bet there's some Viking in your family.

ERIKA. A little Norwegian on both sides. So I guess, yeah.

DONTRELL. Erika. Erika what?

ERIKA. Andersen.

DONTRELL. Erika Andersen. Yeah that's Viking all the way.

ERIKA. Dontrell what?

DONTRELL. Dontrell Jones the Third.

ERIKA. Think you can flip me, Dontrell Jones the Third?
Try.
Try.

> (**DONTRELL** *flips* **ERIKA** *onto her back and straddles her.*)

DONTRELL. You know what you look like right now?

ERIKA. What?

DONTRELL. You look like the whole universe looking back at me.
You look like Fate herself.

ERIKA. Yeah?

DONTRELL. Yeah.

ERIKA. What about my lips?

DONTRELL. I like your lips.

ERIKA. What about my tongue?

DONTRELL. I like the way you speak.

ERIKA. …

I'll be your fate if you'll be mine.

DONTRELL. …

Deal.

> *(They kiss and embrace. They disappear into the sheets.)*

Scene Eight

(The Jones's living room.)

*(*DANIELLE *places a big, round, blue cake on the table.)*

*(*DANIELLE *and* ROBBY *sit at the table.)*

*(*DAD *sits alone behind his door watching TV.)*

ROBBY. You made the shit outa that cake.

DANIELLE. ...

ROBBY. ...

Smells *good.*

DANIELLE. We're not eating 'til everybody gets here.

ROBBY. Everybody's here except D, he wouldn't mind.

DANIELLE. And Shea.

ROBBY. Shea's comin'?

DANIELLE. Is that a problem?

ROBBY. Thought this was for family.

DANIELLE. She's my *cousin* who are you?

ROBBY. Hey, I have a *key* to this house, alright Danielle? That's family.

*(*DAD *comes out of his room and strolls to the table.)*

What's happening, Mr. Jones?

DAD. *("I'm taking this.")* This your plate?

ROBBY. I'm not using it.

*(*DAD *slices and plates a piece of cake for himself.)*

DANIELLE. Dad, we're saving that 'til people get here.

DAD. *(Unperturbed.)* Oh, so I ain't no person, huh?

DANIELLE. We're s'pose to all eat it together.

DAD. Don't tell your mother.

*(*DAD *goes back into his room and closes the door.)*

DANIELLE. ...

ROBBY. ...

*(**MOM** enters. She looks at the cake.)*

DANIELLE. It wasn't Dad.

MOM. …

Where these swimming lessons s'pose to be at?

DANIELLE. He said the beach.

MOM. How much they cost?

DANIELLE. He said free.

MOM. When he comin'?

DANIELLE. Like any second, Mom.

Ma'am. Sorry.

MOM. Well he ain't gonna come in and see me just starin' at the door.

> *(**MOM** grabs a small chunk of cake with her fingers. She exits.)*

ROBBY. *(Reaching for the cake knife.)* Hey, if we diggin' in we diggin' in –

> *(**DANIELLE** grabs the cake knife, **ROBBY** recoils.)*

DANIELLE. Reach for my cake one more again.

ROBBY. Hell no. With your *psycho* eyes.

DANIELLE. Only thing wrong with my eyes,

Is they keepin' watch over people that don't act right.

ROBBY. …

Big bro got you stressin', huh?

DANIELLE. …

ROBBY. Listen, people gonna do what they do.

'Specially your brother.

You were prolly too young to remember this. I was five. So D was four. And we're playin' Power Rangers. We've created this epic wild-animal gladiator battle type scenario, and it's getting kind of intense – so we're on a break. And we're knockin' back some Kool-Aids and whatnot, and allasudden he leans over all secretive and he's like "I'm going to the zoo tomorrow."

And I'm thinkin' – cool. WE goin' to the zoo tomorrow – 'cause you know how I do: I don't like to miss events. So I clear my schedule for the next day.

DANIELLE. Mhmm.

ROBBY. And when I come over here in the morning your mom answers the door and she calls for D, and he doesn't come. And I say, "He's not still sleeping is he? We gotta get to the zoo."

And your mom looks at me like "zoo?"

And I walk with her back to D's room and that little baller has bounced.

I'm sayin' like Kunta Kinte bounced. Forreal. Got up all early, put some miles behind him before the sun came up, this kid was not *playin'*.

And he was actually going the right direction, too, is the crazy thing. 'Cause when the cops finally find him he's like *on the route*.

But I just remember waiting…right here. Lookin' at the door.

Terrified. 'Cause, to me at the time, the dangerous thing about going to the zoo without a grownup was one of the animals would eat you.

So I've got these visions of D like, standing at the snack shop tryna buy a five dollar hotdog and then a bear tackles him and it's over, and I don't have a best friend anymore, you know? And as far as my five-year-old brain is concerned the probability of that happening is like 95% so I'm basically in mourning – and then the door opens and it's your mom and she's got D in her arms and he's lookin' straight up pissed. He's lookin' grown man angry. 'Cause he wasn't finished with his business. Knowhatimsayin', and your mom is just crying and crying 'cause, you know she thought she had lost her baby…

And the only thing I could think was: Dontrell's invincible.

He wrestled the bear and he won.

And he doesn't even have a scratch.

And I've never doubted him and I've never worried about him ever since.

That's on the real.

DANIELLE. …

I wasn't too young.

I remember.

> (**DONTRELL** *and* **ERIKA** *enter through the door. Holding hands. Beaming.*)

ROBBY. 'Sup D.

DONTRELL. Robby Rhymes!

> (**ROBBY** *and* **DONTRELL** *do an elaborate, custom handshake.*)

ERIKA. Hi.

DONTRELL. This is Erika. This is Robby, that's my sister Danielle.

DANIELLE. Hey.

ERIKA. Hi.

ROBBY. What's goin' on.

DANIELLE. *(To* **ERIKA.***)* You hungry?

ERIKA. Oohh brafternoon snack, yes please.

ROBBY. Not cool Danielle!

DANIELLE. *(To* **ERIKA**, *serving her a piece of cake.)* Have a seat.

> *(To* **ROBBY.***)*

Guests eat first, you can't *not* feed a hungry guest.

ERIKA. *(Looking at the cake.)* Are these mermaids?

DANIELLE. It's a mermaid *family*.

ROBBY. *I'm* hungry, why *I* can't be a guest?

DANIELLE. 'Cause you family with your *key*.

ROBBY. Which mermaid am I, then – that's only four mermaids.

DANIELLE. You're the grumpy crab in the background.

DONTRELL. You really *threw down,* huh little sis?

DANIELLE. Been cookin' since I was *one,* ain't no big deal.

ERIKA. I can tell.

ROBBY. *(To* **DANIELLE**.*)* You have *not.*

DANIELLE. *D.*

DONTRELL. Pretty much, yeah.

DANIELLE. Laundry at one and a half.

Basket and soap on top of the dryer, plopped me in a high chair and said figure it out.

That's how you learn.

    *(*MOM *enters.)*

MOM. *(Overly casual.)* Oh, hi Dontrell, ain't seen you in a couple days.

DONTRELL. Hey, Ma.

MOM. *(Registering the cake-eating* **ERIKA**.*)* ...

Hello.

DONTRELL. This Erika, Ma.

ERIKA. I'm Dontrell's swim coach.

MOM. ...

How he doin' so far?

ERIKA. He's amazing.

He's a natural. Truly, I couldn't believe it.

DONTRELL. Ma, it was – Oh my God: Erika has a place down the Bay, right? And we're down there in the water and I wasn't scared at all. Not at all, and I almost drowned at the / pool yesterday –

MOM. You *what?*!

DONTRELL. I tried that sink or swim at the pool and this woman saved my life –

ERIKA. It's no big deal –

DONTRELL. Revived me –

ERIKA. Standard procedure –

DONTRELL. And today it's like I'm a whole different person.

Doggy paddle, scissor kick, breast stroke –

ERIKA. Amazing. Truly amazing.

MOM. …

DONTRELL. So / where's Dad?

MOM. Ain't nobody talkin' to you, Spongebob, pipe down.

> *(To* **ERIKA.***)*

I'm sorry what'd you say your name was?

ERIKA. Erika.

> …

Andersen.

MOM. Ms. Andersen.

> So: You might like to know that your little prodigy here
> happens to be a bonafide and certified wiz kid.
> Straight A's, AP everything. And he only played the
> prissy sports so far as I know he's never been concussed.
> So you would think – having a decent head on his
> shoulders – he'd also have a nice little helping of
> common sense. But such does not seem to be the case.
> Does it?
> 'Cause by my calculations it's T-minus twenty-one days
> 'til classes start, and look I'm all for enjoyment. Enjoy
> your summer days while you can, get outside, ride your
> bike, et cetera, et cetera.
> But see: That?

> *(Points to the scuba gear bag.)*

> That right there has me wonderin'.
> That looks like somethin'. Care to share?

DONTRELL. *(As he opens the bag.)*

> Whoa! Checkthisoutcheckthisout!
> Shea brough this by?

MOM. Mhmmm.

> …

> I don't know, Ms. Andersen.
> Seems like certain people want to keep me in the dark.
> Do you have any light to shed?

And keep in mind that now of all times,

I'm likely to be kind.

Because I have manners. And you're a guest in my house.

DAD. *(Yelling from his room.)* It's my house!

MOM. *(Yelling back at him.)* It's my fuckin' house!

DAD. My motherfuckin' house don't make me say it again!

MOM. Oh hell no it is my house 'cause I make more money than you do, plus I got these two children and your cake stealin' ass to take care of!!

> *(SHEA enters.)*

SHEA. Hey fam, sorry I'm late.

DAD. You just accuse me of *theft* / in my own house?!

MOM. Hell yes I did – hell yes I did go 'head and eat your damn cake!

DAD. Woman I *will* eat my damn cake! I'll eat everyone's cake. I'll eat the platter too if I feel like it. And there ain't shit you can do, cause when a man decides it's time to eat, he gonna *eat*. Tell me I'm wrong.

Tell me I'm wrong and watch me come out there and eat the goddamn table. Gonna taste *good*, too.

ERIKA. *(To SHEA.)* I'm Erika.

DAD. Gonna taste like victory.

SHEA. Hi, I'm Shea.

DONTRELL. Swim coach.

DAD. *(Still making his point.)* Yeah.

That's what I thought!

MOM. The older they get, the more men become their fathers.

And women become their mothers.

That's the way of things Ms. Anderson so I hope you takin' notes.

DONTRELL. Mom that ain't... Hey, I promise Erika, my family ain't normally / like this.

DAD. Yes we are!

ERIKA. It's okay, trust me, my family? Completely dysfunctional.

ROBBY.   **DANIELLE**.

Daaaaaaaaaaaaaamn!   Ohhhhhhhhhhhhhh!

ERIKA. I'm not saying / this is –

MOM. Miss Andersen –

DAD. I'm functioning great! Don't know about y'all.

DONTRELL. We are being kinda dysfunctional right now, Ma.

MOM. And you wouldn't have anything to do with that, because children are *exempt*. Is that what you think?

DANIELLE. Mom, you want some cake?

MOM. Yes, please.

DANIELLE. Y'all ready for cake?

ALL. ["Yes," "Yeah," "Mhmmm," etc.]

>   (**DANIELLE** *begins to pass out plates of cake.*)

MOM. Dontrell Junior come out here and say something to your son, I don't have no words to tell him right now.

>   (**DAD** *briefly comes out of his room.*)

DAD. …

>   Way to go, son. Proud of you.

>   (*Returns to his room.*)

>   (*Silence.*)

MOM. Alright. Everybody raise your plates.

>   Jones family:

>   You who are present,

>   You who are hiding in your dens,

>   You who are no longer with us,

>   Honorary members,

>   Swim coaches.

>   We are here to celebrate the coming of age of a son.

>   And to send him off the proper way.

>   And praise God he's not goin' far.

He's gonna honor us all, by stepping on over to the
very near East and walkin' on that Johns Hopkins real
estate.

What a blessing that is.

And how, how proud we are.

...

(Picks up the wetsuit. To **DONTRELL.***)*

And whatever it is you planning to do with this you may
as well tell us now.

...

DONTRELL. I'd like to get this on the record if I may.

...

(Recorder on.)

I love you all far more than life itself.

Sometimes the things you do for the folks you love,

Sometimes they don't see it. Sometimes they can't.

But you carry them in your heart with every step.

With every breath, with every single thought.

Sometimes there are no words that you can tell them

To make them understand the path you've chosen.

I'm going to the ocean. The Atlantic.

To search for the buried root of my father's tree.

He came to me in a dream two nights ago.

It's my turn to go to him. Simple as that.

Knowing he's out there, where else could I go?

To campus?

Sure, after I've done this.

If it's meant to be.

We are not Destiny's authors. We take notes.

And hope to say we did so faithfully.

(Recorder off.)

MOM. ...

...

I have exercised so much restraint with you, Dontrell.

I have been so patient.

I have –

…

And for what?

For what?

DONTRELL. …

> (**MOM** *takes the cake knife and stabs the wetsuit repeatedly.*)

MOM. *(Stabbing.)* You don't have no sense of duty.
None at all!

DONTRELL. Stop it!

MOM. *(Stabbing.)* You think your dreams the only ones that matter?!

DONTRELL. Ma, stop it!

MOM. *(Stabbing.)* What you think you know about destiny?!
I put my / everything into you boy!

DONTRELL. Ma, stop it! Stop it! Stop it you *bitch*!

> (*Utter silence.*)

> (**DONTRELL** *approaches* **MOM** *and reaches out to touch her.*)

> (**MOM** *pushes him away and his recorder falls on the floor, bursting open.*)

> (**DAD** *opens his door.*)

DAD. Dontrell, come in here.

> (**DONTRELL** *follows* **DAD** *into* **DAD** *'s room.*)

MOM. Party's over, can you all help clean up please?

DANIELLE. Yes ma'am.

> (*All move to help.* **ROBBY** *picks up* **DONTRELL** *'s recorder.*)

MOM. Not you, Erika, you're not family you don't clean up.

ERIKA. I don't mind.

MOM. I do.

> (**DANIELLE, ROBBY,** *and* **SHEA** *exit with dishes.*)

> (**MOM** *sits at the table.*)
>
> (*Holding out her hands.*)

Pray with me, Erika.

> (**ERIKA** *sits and takes* **MOM**'s *hands.*)

ERIKA. ...

> ...

Um.

God...?

MOM. I'm already prayin' don't pray over my prayer.

ERIKA. Sorry.

MOM. Both of us gonna pray silently.

> (**MOM** *and* **ERIKA** *pray silently with their eyes closed.*)
>
> (*In* **DAD**'s *room,* **DAD** *and* **DONTRELL** *stand across from each other.*)

DAD. ...

> ...
>
> ...

DONTRELL. Are you ever gonna say anything?

DAD. I will if I feel like it.

DONTRELL. Yes sir.

DAD. ...

What's goin' on?

DONTRELL. Don't tell me you never had dreams / like I'm talkin' –

DAD. That shit skips a generation.

DONTRELL. Grandpa must've had them, then.

DAD. My old man was a crazy man.

DONTRELL. Did he have dreams like that?

DAD. Like what?

DONTRELL. Vivid.

DAD. Man was a hallucinator, I'm sure he did.

DONTRELL. What'd he hallucinate about?

DAD. Look at you with your questions.

Question every three seconds. I asked you to tell me what's goin' on, you askin' me questions.

…

The dreams you have:

You wake up from 'em?

DONTRELL. Yeah.

DAD. Alright then.

Dreams are dreams. Awake is awake.

Know the difference and you'll be fine.

What else you need to get off your chest?

DONTRELL. Did Grandpa ever say what it was he / hallucinated about?

DAD. Dontrell, did you hear what I said or not?

DONTRELL. I heard you.

DAD. Do you know when you dreamin'? And do you know when you're awake?

DONTRELL. …

Yeah.

DAD. Then you fine. Stay that way so you don't end up in no loony bin.

That's all I got to say about it.

Now: Where you gonna be if you ain't goin' to school?

You gonna start workin'?

You wanna do Military?

DONTRELL. Guess I'd maybe consider the Navy

DAD. Nope, fuck the Navy.

Army.

DONTRELL. How many times have y'all said to me, "Make your own choices, live your own life…"

DAD. That's right, and when you ain't livin' your own life we intervene,

That's our job.

DONTRELL. What?

DAD. We know you, Dontrell.

We know you.

Okay?

We ain't dense.

DONTRELL. I'm tryna learn to scuba dive, Dad.

That's the choice that I made.

DAD. We know.

DONTRELL. And Mom went Mafia on my gear.

DAD. Good.

DONTRELL. Not good.

DAD. And if that makes her a bitch / in your eyes then –

DONTRELL. I shouldn't have said it, okay, that doesn't mean it's right / for her to –

DAD. Right or not right, it's time you learned what a bitch is, boy.

You listenin' to me?

Bitches is Warrior-Women, but we don't know how to call 'em that, and we ain't got no other word for 'em, And yeah, as things are, some of 'em bite. It's a fucked up world, be a man, slap on a band-aid and learn to turn the page.

And make no mistake. Your mother is on your front line, D.

Don't know where you are, but she there. She *been* there. Takin' bullets for you left and right. Bullets you will *never* know about.

Never.

...

Mothers are always on guard. You might think you the protector, might even decide to pack heat, might hire a bodyguard if you can afford it – don't matter. Mamma's gonna still be on guard, because Mamma knows she the last line of defense. Always. No ifs ands or asses – and when the wolves come for ya – And they always come, in one form or another, mark my words,

When you in your darkest hour and them wolves come howlin',

I don't want no pound puppies at the gate. I don't want
no best in show.

I want *Bitches.*

I want *Ruthless Bitches.*

I want *Meeean Bitches* protecting you.

I want Lionesses!

I want Panthers!

I want Mamma Kodiaks rippin' motherfuckers that
come anywhere close!

I want Warrior Women standin' over you!

…

You go out there and kiss your mother.

On the mouth.

And you tell her you ain't goin' near no ocean.

And give her a little peace.

DONTRELL. …

DAD. And give the dead a little peace, too.

DONTRELL. …

DAD. And me a little peace, while you at it.

…

Go kiss your mother.

> (**DONTRELL** *comes out of* **DAD** *'s room and into the
> rest of the house.*)
>
> (**MOM** *and* **ERIKA** *are seated at the table, still
> holding hands in silent prayer.*)
>
> (**DONTRELL** *tries to approach his mother.*)
>
> (*She stops him short with a gesture.*)

MOM. Please don't ask me to buy you a new scuba suit.

…

'Cause I will. Don't ask me, son.

I'd give your body away before I kill your spirit.

But I want both to stick around for awhile.

DONTRELL. …

This ain't what I thought was s'pose to happen,

But you made me realize somethin'.

What I need a suit for?

He didn't have no suit.

He didn't have no gear.

…

What I need more than anything is a boat.

Can you get me a boat?

> *(Unable to answer,* **MOM** *reaches out and tilts* **DONTRELL***'s head up by the chin. She looks at him.)*

> *(***MOM** *kisses* **DONTRELL***.)*

> *(She exits.)*

> *(***DONTRELL** *looks at* **DAD***'s door.)*

> *(***ROBBY** *enters.)*

ROBBY. *(Giving* **DONTRELL** *the recorder.)* Hey man, it still works.

Couple screws.

…

I'ma bounce.

Ain't mad at ya, bro.

…

> *(Re: the recorder.)*

Lookin' forward to hearin' whatever else you lay down on there.

Stay up, alright?

> *(***ROBBY** *exits.)*

> *(***SHEA** *enters. She goes to* **DAD***'s door and knocks.)*

SHEA. Uncle D?

DAD. What you need?

SHEA. Just wanted to say bye.

DAD. Bye.

> *(***SHEA** *goes to* **DONTRELL***.)*

SHEA. Grandpa tried to hijack an oysterman's skipjack.

Down on the bay. Didn't get very far.

That's what sealed it for him.

When the police reined in the boat he screamed like he was possessed.

He jumped in the water and sunk. They rescued him, then put him in the asylum.

He screamed so much, after a week his voice was gone.

So he started writing letters.

He was smart, like you. He should have been a poet.

He suffered there as long as he could bear it.

Then he drowned himself in the tub.

…

We got us a legacy, cousin.

The question is, how do we answer it?

Me?

I go to work.

I tell folks every day: Prepare to be Amazed.

I walk those watery halls.

Sometimes I stay late.

I find my peace.

…

Uncle D has a gift for holding things inside.

What it does to him, I don't know. But that's his way.

And it's his. Not yours to judge.

Danielle: Nonstop drawing mermaids at age seventeen?

She'll figure it out. She's well-balanced, that girl.

…

And you.

…

You'd make a great college student.

You would.

But I don't know if they have anything to teach you.

Do what *you* have to do, Cuz.

No more. And no less.

(SHEA exits.)

(DANIELLE enters.)

DANIELLE. You get any cake, D?

DONTRELL. No.

(DANIELLE feeds DONTRELL one forkful of cake.)

(DANIELLE exits.)

(DONTRELL looks at ERIKA, who has been sitting in silent meditation.)

(They look at each other.)

(They look.)

(They look.)

ERIKA. What are you thinking?

DONTRELL. I don't know.

ERIKA. …

We just sat. Your mom and I.

DONTRELL. Yeah?

ERIKA. And prayed.

I don't pray.

But I did.

And I didn't know what to say. Or think.

So I thought about everything.

My whole life from beginning to now.

It was like a purging. A very sudden, very unexpected *purging*.

I cried. And cried. And cried.

And your mom held my hand. And I cried some more.

And then I was hollow.

And then…

Then I *wasn't*.

DONTRELL. …Like you were full?

ERIKA. Like I suddenly had an awareness.

That last night when we…

(ERIKA holds DONTRELL's head against her belly.)

(They are still.)

(…)

(…)

ERIKA. I have no reference point,
  To say that's what it is.
  But that's what it is.
  That's what it is, Dontrell.

DONTRELL. Oh.

ERIKA. And I don't feel at all worried.
  We said we'd be each other's fate.

DONTRELL. Yeah.

ERIKA. And this is Fate saying, "Okay."

DONTRELL. Yeah.

ERIKA. Yeah.

DONTRELL. …
  Maybe I should scale it back.

ERIKA. What?

DONTRELL. Recoup?
  Start school?

ERIKA. Dontrell –

DONTRELL. Estimate some coordinates maybe somehow?
  Give my family a little time?
  I mean it's kind of a big crazy thing to do, maybe we all
  just need to adjust to the idea.

ERIKA. You think it's crazy?

DONTRELL. Well, yeah.
  No, not like *crazy*, crazy,
  More like "crazy."

ERIKA. Well I disagree.
  I believe in you.
  Completely.
  …
  And belief is a deed.
  And trust is a deed.

And love is a deed.

Isn't it?

DONTRELL. ...

ERIKA. Meet me down at my place tomorrow morning. On the beach.

Will you?

DONTRELL. ...

ERIKA. Will you?

DONTRELL. ...

>   (*ERIKA exits.*)
>
>   (*Recorder on.*)

...

...

...

>   (*Recorder off.*)
>
>   (**DAD** *comes into the living room with a pair of very old shoes.*)
>
>   (**COMPANY** *pounds the floor as* **DAD** *walks.*)

COMPANY. (*Thud!*)

>   (*Thud!*)
>
>   (*Thud!*)
>
>   (*Thud!*)
>
>   (*Thud!*)

DAD. Wherever it is you end up going: Walk in these. They're your grandfather's.

>   (**DAD** *puts the shoes down. He exits.* **DONTRELL** *picks up the shoes.*)
>
>   (*He tries to slip one on. It's blocked by balled-up papers. He pulls out the papers. He opens one. Smooths it out. He opens another...*)
>
>   (*The papers are, in fact, letters.*)
>
>   (**DONTRELL** *begins to read.*)

DONTRELL. Dontrell Jones.

...

"If I am a madman, as sane men say I am,

ALL COMPANY. Then what I write is of no consequence.

SHEA. And if my words are of no consequence,

DAD. Then I beg this ink to sing,

DANIELLE. Or dance,

MOM. Or shimmer,

DAD. By some light I cannot see from here,

ALL COMPANY. And say what I cannot,

DONTRELL. And speak to those who follow after me,

SHEA. And tell them that to suffer is to live.

DANIELLE. And tell them that when I have pulled out my hair,

DAD. And screamed away my voice,

ROBBY. And rent my clothes,

MOM. It is because the Spirit Beneath the Sea,

ALL COMPANY. A long lost father of my line,

DONTRELL. Remains there in the deep, while I am here.

SHEA. I wish my veins were rivers to the ocean,

DAD. And my surging heart a bay.

MOM. My sanity proclaims that blood is but blood,

DANIELLE. And hearts are hearts,

ROBBY. And what is lost is lost,

SHEA. And by that logic, I am driven mad.

DONTRELL. Forgive me, future, what I have left undone.
Forgive me, that I never learned to swim.
How strange: A wanderer on life's sea, who cannot swim."

...

　　　(**DONTRELL** *turns his recorder on.*)

Future Generations:

　　　(**DONTRELL** *holds the recorder to his heart.*)

ALL COMPANY. Bum-bum!
 Bum-bum!
 Bum-bum!
 Bum-bum!
 Bum-bum!

Scene Nine

(Erika's apartment. Night.)

*(**ERIKA** sits by her window. She looks into her mirror. Her makeup case sits on the table in front of her.)*

ERIKA. Is it strange that when I look in Grandma's little mirror I see me,
but when I look in my own mirror I see you?
You'd think it'd be the other way around.
Well, Mom.

...

Thank you for the makeup even though I actually mostly stole it.
You gave me what you could.

...

Thank you for this opportunity you have given me.
To reinvent myself.

...

You can never be too good for your own family.
You have to take their gifts.
And make them yours.

(She dips her fingers into the makeup case and begins applying blue war paint to her face...)

One line to remember,
Another to forget.
Three to call the rains down.
Four to stay adrift.

Scene Ten

(A Viking longship appears onstage.)

(Perhaps it is brought on or assembled by the **COMPANY**. *Perhaps it appears magically from above or below. Perhaps it is beautifully detailed, magnificent and elaborate. Perhaps it is simple. Perhaps it is just a sail and some music.)*

(In any case, this is a monumental event.)

*(***ERIKA**, *who has remained onstage, crosses to the boat.)*

*(***DONTRELL**, *who has entered during the transition, meets her. They are at the beach. The boat is docked.)*

DONTRELL. …

   …

   …

   …

ERIKA. Right?

DONTRELL. This yours?

ERIKA. Ours.

DONTRELL. …

   My God.

ERIKA. The duncle delivers!

   I said look, Dad – I called him Dad! – I said if you insist on giving me *gifts*, there's only one thing I need. And I need it right now.

   He was actually pretty psyched about it.

   We had the longest conversation we've ever had.

   He's getting really into his heritage now.

   This is a scaled down version of a *snekkja*. Which is a kind of Viking longship.

   I mean this one's more in the artisan interpretation realm, but it floats and it rows, so…

DONTRELL. *(Recorder on.)* Captain's Log: We have our vessel.

ERIKA. It's supposed to be in great condition, I didn't tell
    him of course that I was planning on taking it *out* out,
    you know, far.

    But water is water, right?

DONTRELL. *(Still recording.)* She's a beauty.

    The skies are clear as mirrors, the air is fresh.

> *(Recorder off.)*

After you, my love.

ERIKA. You first.

> (**DONTRELL** *climbs into the boat.* **ERIKA** *follows.*)
>
> *(The* **COMPANY** *now exits the stage entirely,
> leaving* **DONTRELL** *and* **ERIKA** *alone in the boat.*)

DONTRELL. *(Recorder on.)* Future Generations: We've come
    a long way together,

    Haven't we?

    It's been quite a journey, hasn't it?

    Well now it's time for destinations.

    If prayers are eternal, future,

    Pray for us now.

    And keep 'em comin'.

> *(Recorder off.)*

. . .

> *(To* **ERIKA**.*)*

Row with me a bit?

> (**ERIKA** *and* **DONTRELL** *row.*)
>
> *(They row.)*
>
> *(They row.)*
>
> *(They row.)*
>
> *(They take a deep breath together.)*

ERIKA. The threshold where the bay gives itself to the
    ocean.

> *(They begin rowing again.)*

DONTRELL. Wind in our hair. And what is wind?

ERIKA. The earth blowing you a long kiss.

DONTRELL. Invigorating you.

ERIKA. Your oars find their rhythm.

DONTRELL. They play with the waves.

ERIKA. Each stroke more efficient.

DONTRELL. You coast.

> (**DONTRELL** *and* **ERIKA** *raise their oars out of the water.*)

ERIKA. You glide.

DONTRELL. The horizon is,

ERIKA. Two blue pearls:

DONTRELL. The sky,

ERIKA. And the sea,

DONTRELL. And one may as well be the other.

ERIKA. No shore in sight.

DONTRELL. Inches and miles,

ERIKA. Are hard to distinguish.

Hours pass like seconds,

DONTRELL. And when the stars come out,

ERIKA. You want to cry. So beautiful,

DONTRELL. Is the logic of the heavens.

> (**DONTRELL** *and* **ERIKA** *look up. They shift their oars in unison as they gaze at the sky.*)

DONTRELL & ERIKA. East.

   …

A little South.

   …

East.

> *(They coast.)*
> *(Coasting.)*
> *(…)*
> *(…)*

(Coasting on the new moon sea.)

(…)

(…)

DONTRELL. Our child should learn to swim early.
Water birth, and from there, sky's the limit.
He or she won't have to come way out here.
No loose ends to knot up.
He or she might find a whole new way of swimming.
A whole new way of being, maybe.

ERIKA. I hope so.

(They row.)

(They row.)

(They row.)

(They row.)

(They row.)

The waves are getting high.

DONTRELL. High seas ain't no lie!

ERIKA. Is it a storm?

DONTRELL. Don't think so.

ERIKA. What then?

DONTRELL. Row into it.

(They row.)

(They row.)

(They row.)

(They row.)

(They row.)

Miles in front of us,

ERIKA. And behind.

DONTRELL. Treacherous waters,

ERIKA. Only carry us faster.

*(**DONTRELL** and **ERIKA** again change directions, moving their oars in unison, looking up.)*

DONTRELL. A little more south.

ERIKA. East.

DONTRELL. South.

ERIKA. Row.

DONTRELL. Row.

ERIKA. Row.

DONTRELL & ERIKA. Coast.

     (They coast.)

ERIKA. Do you think we're getting close? To anything?

DONTRELL. Closer than we were.

    Row.

ERIKA. Just keep going?

    Row.

DONTRELL. Until forever becomes forever, if we have to.

    Row.

ERIKA. There's no other choice.

    Row. Row.

DONTRELL. We left choice on the shore.

    Row. Row. Row.

ERIKA. If we knew what our vows would make us do.

    Row. Row. Row.

DONTRELL. We'd never, ever, ever, ever, make them.

    Row.

     (They coast.)

ERIKA. I know this is gonna sound really, really, corny:

DONTRELL. *Corny.* Pshh. That's a word for land-dwellers. Crop growers. We're sea people, you and I.

ERIKA. Well I was just thinking about how people say their love is bigger than the ocean…

DONTRELL. Uhuh…

ERIKA. And I was just looking around and I was like: Man. That's really big.

     (They begin laughing…)

DONTRELL. *(Crawling over to* **ERIKA**.*)* Wait, stay there, don't move.

ERIKA. Where am I gonna go?

> *(The laughing escalates...)*

Are you crawling over here to kiss me?

DONTRELL. Yes!

ERIKA. Why?

DONTRELL. I can't row anymore! My arms don't work.

ERIKA. Mine neither!

DONTRELL. My lips work, though. I think.

ERIKA. Mine too! Mine too!

> *(They kiss a few times. They lie down in exhaustion.)*

Let's sing a lullaby to the baby.

DONTRELL. Okay.

ERIKA. What should we sing?

DONTRELL. All I can think of right now is "Row Row Row Your Boat."

ERIKA. Let's not sing that.

DONTRELL. Okay.

ERIKA. ...

Think of something.

> *(The Ocean begins to hum.)*
>
> *(The humming of the Ocean becomes louder and louder.)*
>
> *(The humming is coming from the* **COMPANY**.*)*
>
> *(They hum.)*
>
> *(They sigh.)*
>
> *(They clap.)*
>
> *(They stomp.)*
>
> *(They hum all the while.)*
>
> *(They surround* **DONTRELL** *and* **ERICA**.*)*

DONTRELL. *(Recorder on.)* Captain's Log: Future Generations:

I do not know our longitude or latitude.
I do not know the time.
I do not know the day.
An ocean of light is all I see.

>*(Recorder off.)*

>*(**DONTRELL** and **ERIKA** look over the ship's edge.)*

>*(The Ocean goes silent.)*

>*(**DONTRELL** holds up a stack of his grandfather's letters. He has flattened them out and bound them with a rubber band.)*

ERIKA. What are those?

DONTRELL. Offerings. Letters. Very dear to me.
And I hope to him as well.

>*(As if tossing seeds onto fertile soil, **DONTRELL** scatters the letters into the sea.)*

>*(To the Ocean.)*

Come up, and come aboard!

>*(**ERIKA** and **DONTRELL** wait.)*

>*(Nothing happens.)*

>*(**DONTRELL** pulls his grandfather's shoes off his feet. He gives one to **ERIKA**.)*

>*(They toss the shoes into the sea.)*

>*(To the Ocean.)*

We ask you to come aboard! To come with us to shore!

>*(Nothing happens.)*

>*(Recorder on.)*

Future generations:
I am sorry, but I have to let you go.
I hoped you would remember my name.
But what are names?
The symbols of ourselves.
We may yet be without them.

(**DONTRELL** *drops his recorder into the sea.*)

DONTRELL. Come aboard.

(*Nothing happens.*)

...

...

...

(**DONTRELL** *looks to his right. Then to his left. He springs into the deep.*)

(**DONTRELL** *swims down.*)

(*Down.*)

(*Down.*)

(*Down.*)

SHEA. Bum-bum.

MOM. Bum-bum.

DANIELLE. Heart-beat.

ALL COMPANY. Heart-beat-heart-beat-heart-beat.

ROBBY. Beat.

SHEA. Beat.

ALL COMPANY. Deeper. Deeper.

DANIELLE. Deep.

MOM. Deep.

SHEA. Darkness.

(*Dontrell's* **ANCESTOR** *enters. He is part man, part ocean spirit.*)

(*The* **ANCESTOR** *stands, looking at* **DONTRELL**.)

ANCESTOR. Kini oruku e?* [What is your name?]

DONTRELL. ...

ANCESTOR. Kini oruku e?

...

Ilu wo lo ti wa? [What place are you from?]

---

*__ANCESTOR__'s lines are spoken in Yoruba. The English translations [in brackets] are not spoken.

DONTRELL. ...

ANCESTOR. Ta ni e ti o n peja fun oku? [Who are you that comes fishing for the dead?]

...

> (**ANCESTOR** *approaches* **DONTRELL.** **ANCESTOR** *reaches out, touching* **DONTRELL** *'s face.*)

Nje o ki n se eran ara mi? [Is this not my flesh?]

...

Nje o ki n se eje mi? [Is this not my blood?]

...

> (**ANCESTOR** *gestures upward. Indicating that it is time for* **DONTRELL** *to go.*)
>
> (**DONTRELL** *declines.*)
>
> (**ANCESTOR** *gestures up again.*)
>
> (**DONTRELL** *opens his mouth to answer and the ocean rushes in.*)
>
> (**DONTRELL** *passes out.*)

A o Jo maa lo. [We shall all go with you.]

> (*More* **ANCESTORS** *emerge: All remaining members of the* **COMPANY**.*)
>
> (*Swelling music*, as they enter, dancing. It is the dance of Yemaya, Goddess of the Ocean.*)
>
> (*Their garments are like the waves of the ocean. Their faces and bodies are streaked in blue.*)
>
> (*Dancing.*)
>
> (*Dancing.*)
>
> (*Dancing.*)
>
> (*As the dance picks up energy and intensity,* **DONTRELL** *rises. He joins in the dance.*)
>
> (*He dances.*)

---

*Licensees should create original music or use music in the public domain.

(He dances.)

(DONTRELL *is lifted back into the boat, where he stands beside* **ERIKA. ANCESTOR** *stands with them.)*

(Gathered in and around the boat, the **COMPANY** *stomps on the ground, four times.)*

COMPANY. *(Thud.)*

...

(Thud.)

...

(Thud.)

...

(Thud.)

End of Play